Kim R. Stafford

We Got Here Together

ILLUSTRATED BY

Debra Frasier

Harcourt Brace & Company

SAN DIEGO   NEW YORK   LONDON

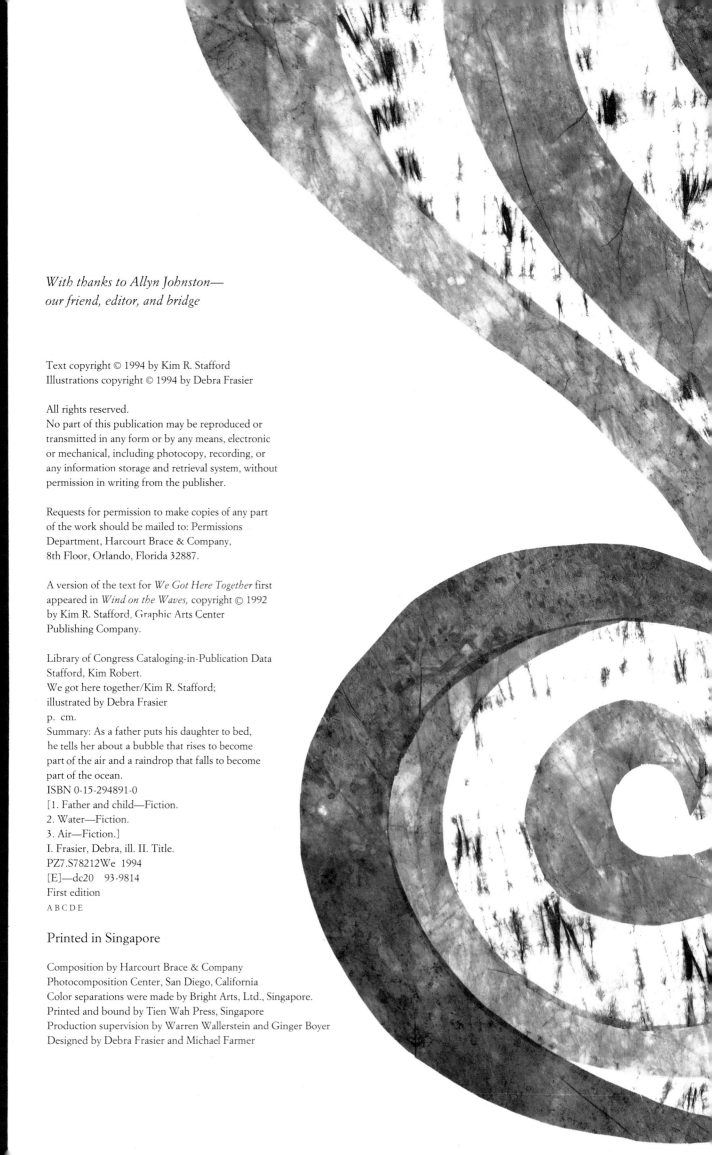

With thanks to Allyn Johnston—
our friend, editor, and bridge

Text copyright © 1994 by Kim R. Stafford
Illustrations copyright © 1994 by Debra Frasier

A version of the text for *We Got Here Together* first
appeared in *Wind on the Waves,* copyright © 1992
by Kim R. Stafford, Graphic Arts Center
Publishing Company.

Library of Congress Cataloging-in-Publication Data
Stafford, Kim Robert.
We got here together/Kim R. Stafford;
illustrated by Debra Frasier
p. cm.
Summary: As a father puts his daughter to bed,
he tells her about a bubble that rises to become
part of the air and a raindrop that falls to become
part of the ocean.
ISBN 0-15-294891-0
[1. Father and child—Fiction.
2. Water—Fiction.
3. Air—Fiction.]
I. Frasier, Debra, ill. II. Title.
PZ7.S78212We 1994
[E]—dc20 93-9814
First edition
A B C D E

Printed in Singapore

Composition by Harcourt Brace & Company
Photocomposition Center, San Diego, California
Color separations were made by Bright Arts, Ltd., Singapore.
Printed and bound by Tien Wah Press, Singapore
Production supervision by Warren Wallerstein and Ginger Boyer
Designed by Debra Frasier and Michael Farmer

For the song of water,
rising and falling

Now you get settled in bed,
I'll tell you a story.

You get cozy, and I'll start.

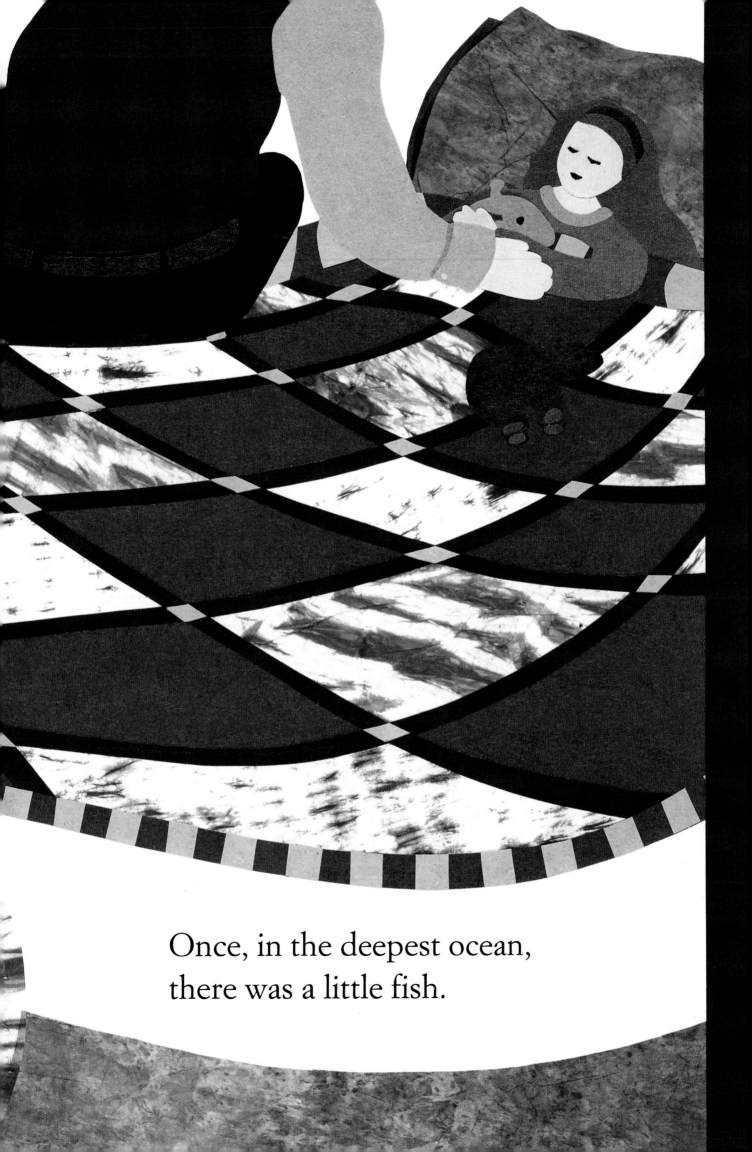

Once, in the deepest ocean,
there was a little fish.

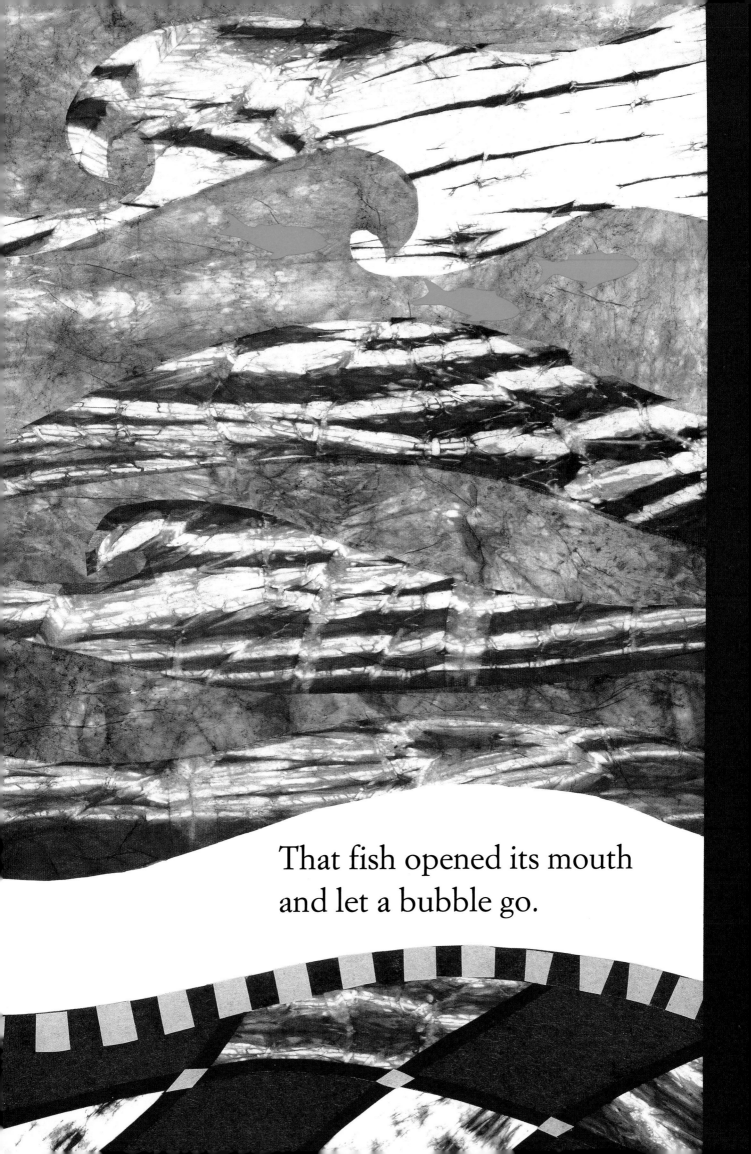

That fish opened its mouth
and let a bubble go.

At the same moment
a cloud high over the ocean
let a raindrop go.

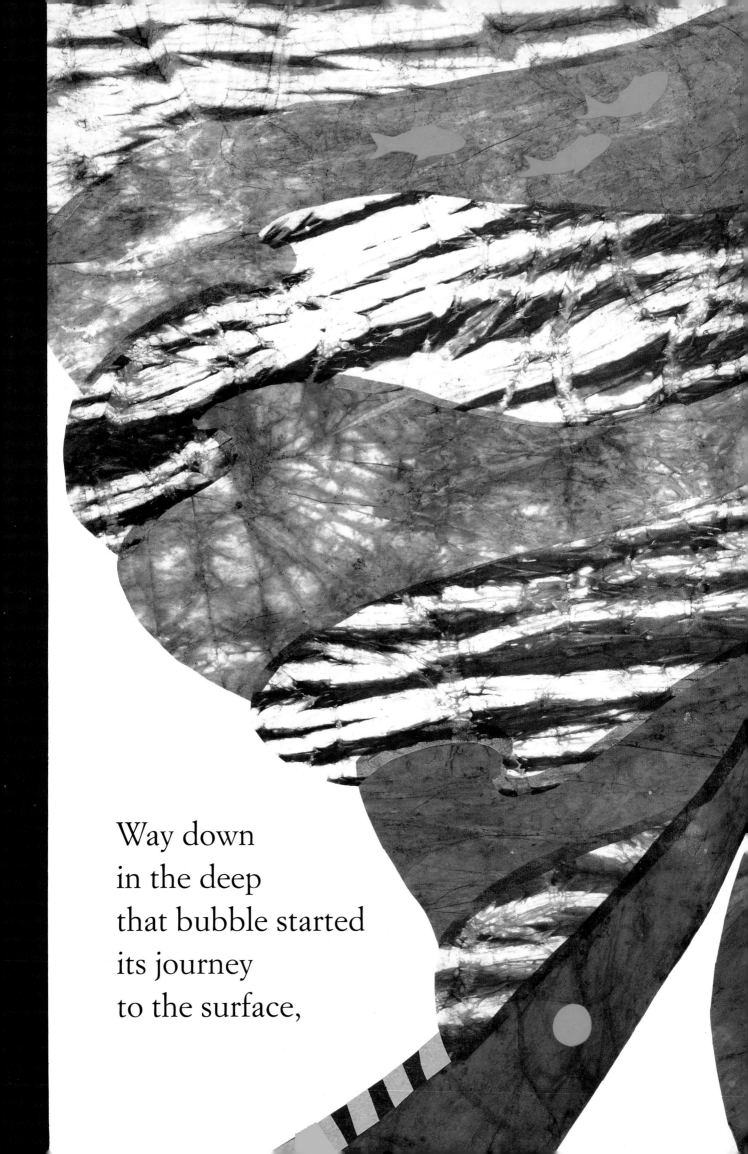

Way down
in the deep
that bubble started
its journey
to the surface,

and high in the sky
that raindrop
started down.

Would you be afraid?
I might be afraid.

But nothing can hurt a raindrop,
nothing can hurt a bubble.

They belong where they're going.

For a long time that bubble drifted up through the water without a thought,

bumping a seal belly,

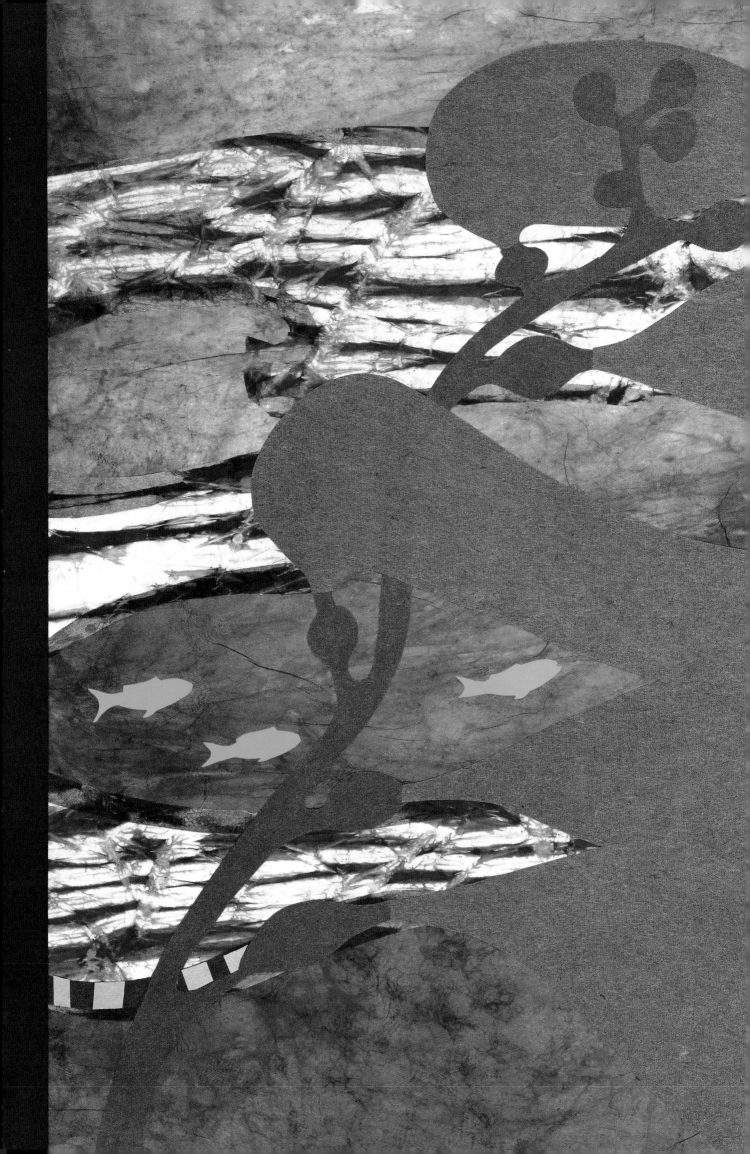

bouncing off a seaweed leaf,

rolling through the blue, floating
toward that big ceiling of light.

And the raindrop was spinning
dizzy down,

sliding along the shoulder
of the wind, tumbling toward
that silver field of water.

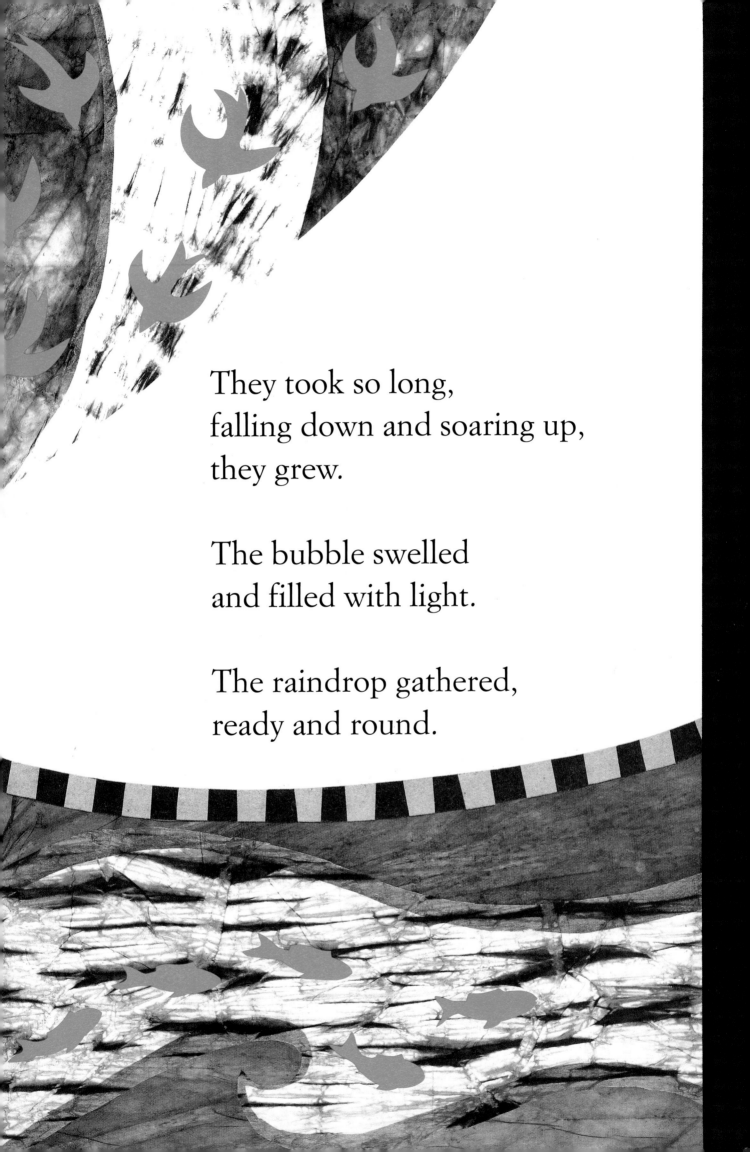

They took so long,
falling down and soaring up,
they grew.

The bubble swelled
and filled with light.

The raindrop gathered,
ready and round.

Somehow they were aimed
for the exact same moment in time,
and they got there together.

Then they were—what were they?

The bubble opened
and was the whole sky.

The raindrop opened
and was the whole ocean.

There they were—
sky and ocean turning
right where they belonged.

And you and I?

We got here together, too,
didn't we?

We got here safe,
in the silver light,
where we belong.

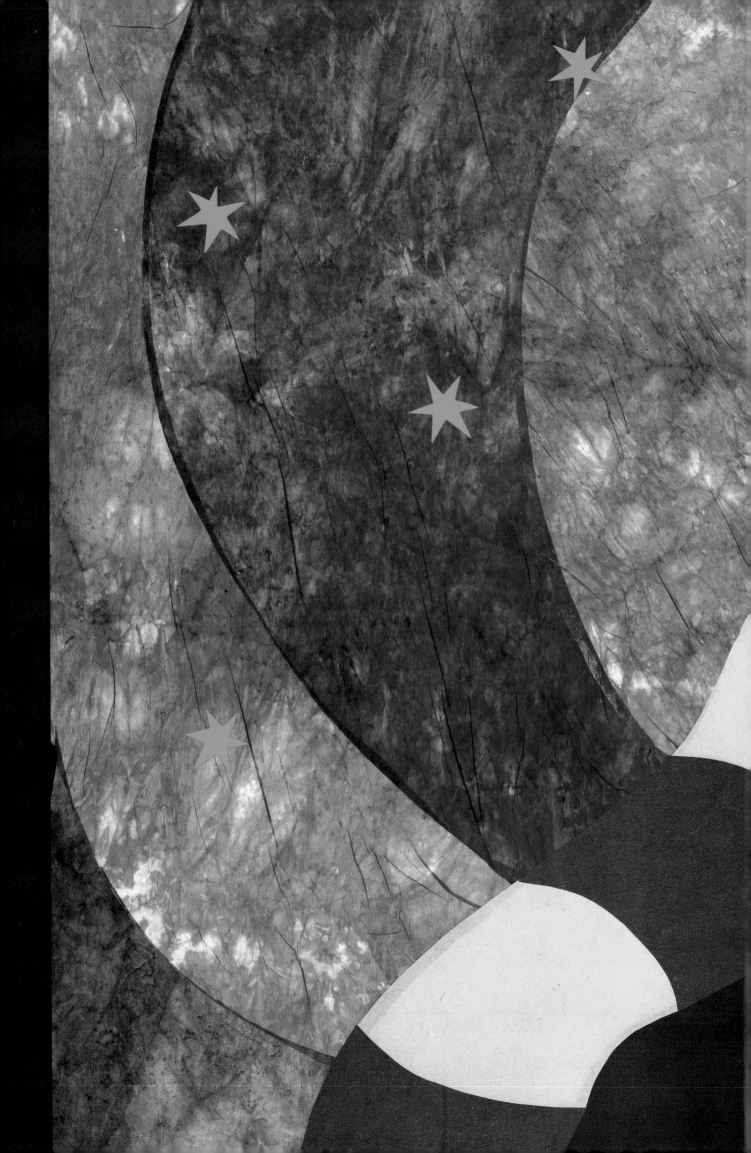

ILLUSTRATOR'S NOTE

The patterned papers in this book were dyed in the *shibori* style, a traditional Japanese resist process usually reserved for cloth. For the ocean papers, each sheet was rolled around a large pipe, wrapped with a string, and dipped into indigo dye. The string resists the dye and, when removed, leaves an irregular white line that looks surprisingly like moving water. Before the sky papers were dyed, they were cut into narrow strips and braided tightly. When they were unbraided, the resulting fine-lined pattern on them reminded me of falling rain.

From the beginning it seemed important to make the papers for this book with the help of water.

—D.F.

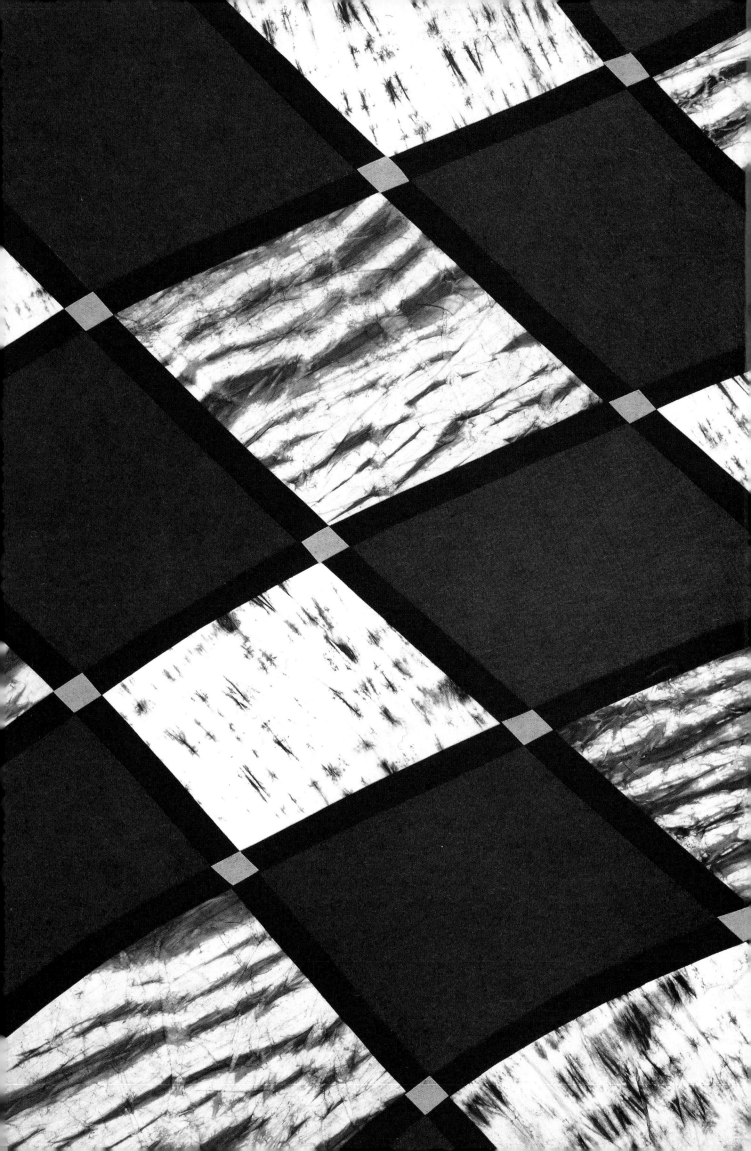